FULL WORM MOON

MARGO LEMIEUX · PICTURES BY ROBERT ANDREW PARKER

NAPERVILLE PUBLIC LIBRARIES
Naperville, Illinois

Tambourine Books 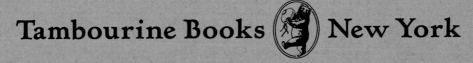 New York

Text copyright © 1994 by Marguerite G. Fisher

Illustrations copyright © 1994 by Robert Andrew Parker

All rights reserved. No part of this book may be reproduced or utilized in any form or by any means, electronic or mechanical, including photocopying, recording, or by any information storage or retrieval system, without permission in writing from the Publisher. Inquiries should be addressed to Tambourine Books, a division of William Morrow & Company, Inc., 1350 Avenue of the Americas, New York, New York 10019. Printed in Singapore. Book design by Golda Laurens. The text is set in Hadriano Light. The illustrations were painted in watercolor on paper.

Library of Congress Cataloging in Publication Data

Lemieux, Margo. Full worm moon/by Margo Lemieux; illustrated by Robert Andrew Parker.—1st ed. p. cm. Summary: An Algonquian family spends a cold night waiting to see the earthworms dance as they did in the ancient story about the full worm moon. 1. Algonquian Indians—Juvenile fiction. [1. Algonquian Indians—Fiction. 2. Indians of North America—Fiction.] I. Parker, Robert Andrew, ill. II. Title. PZ7.L537377Fu 1994 [E]—dc20 93-14728 CIP AC   ISBN 0-688-12105-5.—ISBN 0-688-12106-3 (lib. bdg.)   First edition 10 9 8 7 6 5 4 3 2 1

To my mother, Geraldine Juliette Lemieux, for her faith in me.
And thank you to Philip and Eleanor Brady, Nanepashemet,
and Anita Nielsen for their advice and expertise.
M.L.

To Willem and Max, Russell and Jack, and Reed.
R.A.P.

"Tell us. Tell us again about the worms," Atuk said to his mother, Monamie.

Monamie laughed as she stirred the pot of beans. "I have been telling you the story all winter long. You know the story better than I. You should be telling me."

"Tell us, tell us," Atuk and his sister, Mequin, chanted.

A blast of cold air announced the arrival of Atuk's father, Anawan. As he burst into the smoky wigwam, the fire wavered and quivered, and shadows leapt across the walls.

"The ice on the lake is starting to thaw," he said, holding up fish that gleamed silver in the firelight. "We will have a treat tonight."

"Atuk and Mequin want to hear the legend of the Full Worm Moon again," said Mother.

Anawan was thoughtful. "Tonight is the night of the Full Worm Moon. I have never seen the worms. Maybe we could watch for them."

"I want to see them," said Atuk.

"Me too, me too," cried Mequin.

Monamie said, "We would have to spend the night on the cold ground in order to see them."

"We can do it. Please. Please," shouted the children.

"Then we will," said Father, laughing.

Atuk hardly tasted the fish-and-bean stew, he was so eager.

As soon as the meal was over, Átuk and Mequin rolled up the warm elk-skin robes. The family left the wigwam just as the sun set and the moon appeared in the east.

"Here is a good spot," said Father. "We must keep a close watch."

"Tell us the story again," pleaded Átuk as he and Mequin curled up in their robes.

"Very well," said Mother, only her eyes visible. "Long, long ago, the earthworms helped the People by burrowing and softening the soil, preparing for planting the golden corn, the rich, sweet squash, the crisp beans. The worms did such a good job that the People didn't need to prepare the soil. They just watched and ate, becoming fat and lazy. The Sun was not pleased. He went to the edge of the sky to think."

"What happened?" Atuk and Mequin chanted eagerly.

Mother smiled. "What happens when you go away from the fire?"

"We get cold," Mequin cried.

"Ssssh," said Atuk. His toes were chilly. His breath made a little cloud.

"Yes. While the Sun was far away, the world was very cold. The leaves turned colors and fell from the trees. Ice froze the rivers and lakes. The soil hardened. The People became thin.

"A wise old man said, 'The Sun is angry. If we share the work with the earthworms, maybe he will return.' The man climbed the highest hill to call the Sun but he was too far away.

"The wise man meditated. He said, 'We will ask his sister, the Moon, to talk to him. Moon is closer to him than we are.'

"When the Moon appeared as she always did at night, the wise man pleaded, 'Tell the Sun we are sorry. We want him to return.'

"The Moon delivered the message and the Sun replied, 'If the People promise to share the work, I will return. Every year I will send a message with Moon. The full Moon will signal the worms to come from the ground. Once again they will prepare the soil for planting. And I will not be far behind.'

"Now the turning of the seasons is marked by the earthworms' return from their underground shelters. They wiggle to the surface and dance joyfully under the full moon. The next day little mounds of dirt dot the fields where each worm has burrowed out. The farmer knows it is time to work.

"That is why at this time of the year, the full moon is known as the Full Worm Moon."

"I've never seen them dance," whispered Father, "but I hear they dress in red and gold. They have no need of torches because the moonbeams are so bright. They have no need of drums because music comes from the air."

Cold began to bite Átuk's toes and ears but he sat straight and alert.

"Are you sleepy?" asked Father.

"No," replied Átuk.

"Are you cold?"

"No." But the ground was very hard. The earthworms were taking a long time to come out.

"Are you sleepy or cold?" Father asked again.

"No," he replied. "Only a little."

"Me too," said Mequin.

The moon floated higher. Átuk watched intently but the frost was sneaking under his robe.

"I am getting cold," Father whispered. "If you were to come under here with us, I would not be so cold."

Atuk and Mequin quickly scrambled under Anawan's arms and curled up, one on each side, warm and cozy beneath the big elk-skin robe.

"I am getting sleepy," said Mother. "Lean against me so I won't tip over if I fall asleep."

Atuk and Mequin leaned against Father and Mother.

Soon Átuk lost sight of the moon, lost sight of the silvery fields and black branches. He dreamed of worms wearing bright shirts and dancing to music that came from the air.

Átuk opened his eyes.

He heard the rustle of bare branches stirred by midnight air. He heard his parents' quiet breathing. He heard Mequin's quick breath. He heard—

So very faint, from far, far away, Átuk heard drum beats. No—but yes, the faint pulsing of dancing drums floated in the frosty air.

"Listen," Átuk whispered.

"I hear it," Mequin said. "I see them."

Átuk squinted his eyes. The bright patches on the field quivered ever so slightly. "I see them. I see them," he cried.

"Ssssh," said Father. "We don't want to frighten them."

Atuk's eyes grew tired from watching the field. His ears strained to hear the drums. He closed his eyes for just a moment and when he opened them, the sky was pink.

"Mother, Father, Mequin," he cried. "The moon is gone. The worms are gone."

They stood up, stretched, and walked down the hill. Little mounds of new earth were everywhere.

"Time for us to begin planting," said Father. "The sun will soon be back to warm the earth."

"I saw the worms, I saw the worms," Mequin chanted.

"I saw them too," Atuk chimed in.

Father laughed. "We will come next year to see them again. But now we will go back to the wigwam, warm ourselves before the fire, and have a good breakfast."

Author's Note

Full Worm Moon is an original story that tells of how a New England Algonquian family may have lived before the arrival of the Pilgrims.

The people who inhabited this country before the Europeans came lived close to nature and counted months by the full moons. Each full moon had a name that was associated with a natural event at that time of the year, such as the Full Snow Moon or the Full Harvest Moon.

The Full Worm Moon occurs in March when the sunlight is getting stronger and the frozen ground begins to thaw. You can tell the worms have begun to come awake when you find little curly mounds of dirt on the ground. These mounds, or *castings*, are part of nature's way of preparing the earth for new growth. Then the flowers and trees and green grass suddenly burst out and let us know spring is here.